Mr. Monkey
Bakes a Cake

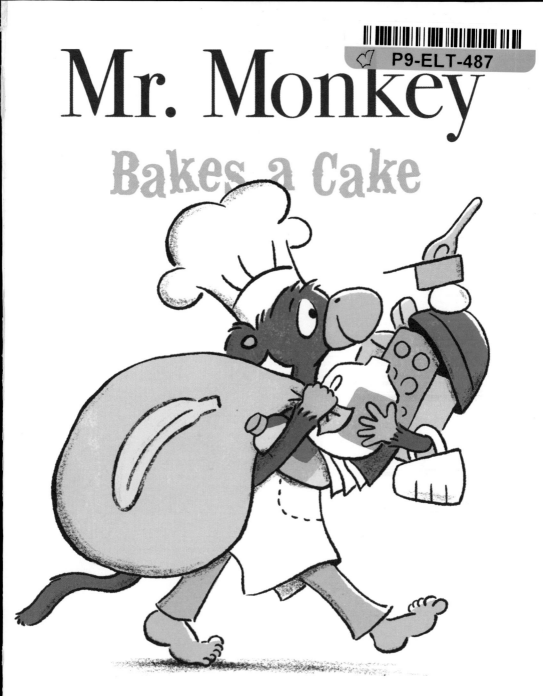

Jeff Mack

Simon & Schuster Books for Young Readers
NEW YORK   LONDON   TORONTO   SYDNEY   NEW DELHI

For Graham. Ooh!

SIMON & SCHUSTER BOOKS FOR YOUNG READERS
An imprint of Simon & Schuster Children's Publishing Division
1230 Avenue of the Americas, New York, New York 10020
Copyright © 2018 by Jeff Mack
For information about special discounts for bulk purchases, please contact Simon & Schuster
Special Sales at 1-866-506-1949 or business@simonandschuster.com.
The Simon & Schuster Speakers Bureau can bring authors to your live event.
For more information or to book an event, contact the Simon & Schuster Speakers Bureau
at 1-866-248-3049 or visit our website at www.simonspeakers.com.
Also available in a Simon & Schuster Books for Young Readers hardcover edition.
Book design by Chloë Foglia and Jeff Mack
The text for this book was set in Century Schoolbook.
The illustrations for this book were rendered digitally.
Manufactured in China
0919 SCP
First Simon & Schuster Books for Yong Readers paperback edition December 2019
2 4 6 8 10 9 7 5 3 1
Library of Congress Cataloging-in-Publication Data
Names: Mack, Jeff, author, illustrator.
Title: Mr. Monkey bakes a cake / Jeff Mack.
Other titles: Mister Monkey bakes a cake
Description: First edition. | New York : Simon & Schuster Books for Young Readers, [2018] | Series: Mr.
Monkey | Summary: Mr. Monkey bakes a cake and enters it in a contest, but nothing goes as planned.
Identifiers: LCCN 2017023009 | ISBN 9781534404311 (hardcover) | ISBN 9781534404328 (eBook)
ISBN 9781534466708 (pbk)
Subjects: | CYAC: Monkeys—Fiction. | Cake—Fiction. | Contests—Fiction. | Humorous stories.
Classification: LCC PZ7.H83727 Mrd 2018 | DDC [E]—dc23
LC record available at https://lccn.loc.gov/2017023009

Mr. Monkey makes a cake.

He adds sugar.

He adds an egg.

He adds bananas.

That's okay.
Monkeys like bananas.

Mr. Monkey
mixes the cake.

Mr. Monkey
bakes the cake.

Mr. Monkey frosts the cake.

Good job, Mr. Monkey!
Now you can eat your cake!

Oh no!
Mr. Monkey ate too many bananas.

That's okay.
Mr. Monkey has a new plan for his cake.

Mr. Monkey wants to win that ribbon.
But first . . .

how about one more banana?

Mr. Monkey saves the banana for later.

Good idea!

Mr. Monkey walks to the cake show.

He walks . . .

and he walks.

Mr. Monkey
waits.

He waits . . .

and he waits.

Walk, Mr. Monkey!

Wait, Mr. Monkey!

Nice catch, Mr. Monkey!

Uh-oh!
More trouble.

The cake is safe.

Mr. Monkey hides.

Mr. Monkey runs.

The cake is safe.

Or is it?

Mr. Monkey runs.

Mr. Monkey hides.

GRR!

Or is it?

Mr. Monkey runs!

Mr. Monkey arrives at the cake show.

It wasn't easy, but the cake is safe.

Mr. Monkey is in luck.

The cake is still safe.

It's time to win that ribbon!

Oh no!
The cake show is over.
Everyone already won a ribbon.

Everyone but Mr. Monkey.

Poor Mr. Monkey.
How could this day get any worse?

Run, Mr. Monkey!

Run!

Hide, Mr. Monkey!

Hide!

Mr. Monkey is trapped!

There is nowhere to run.

There is nowhere to hide.

What will he do?

Good idea!
Gorillas like bananas too.

Look!
Mr. Monkey has a new friend . . .

But wait!

Now someone else
doesn't have a ribbon.

Good job, Mr. Monkey!

Now you can have your cake
and eat it too!